Magic Ballerina™

Rosa and the Golden Bird

Darcey Bussell

HarperCollins *Children's Books*

*To Phoebe and Zoe, as they are the inspiration
behind Magic Ballerina.*

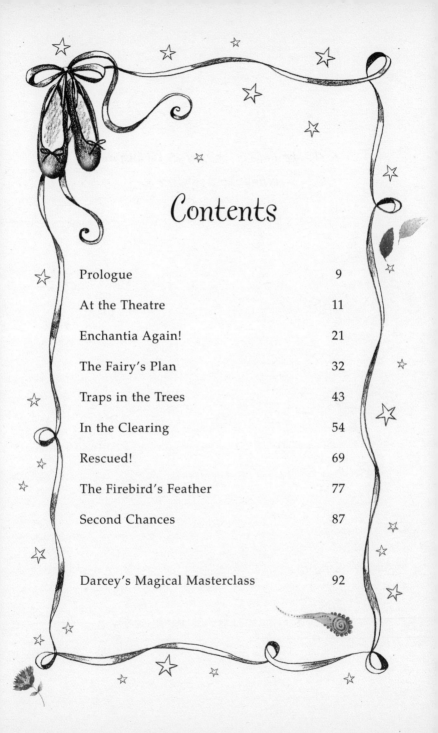

Contents

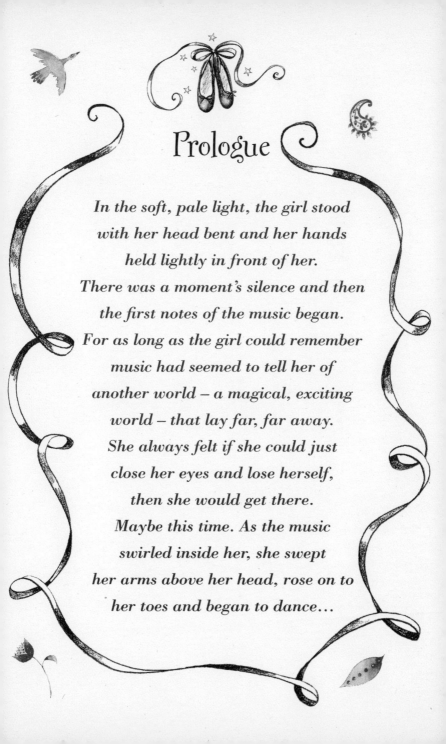

Prologue

*In the soft, pale light, the girl stood
with her head bent and her hands
held lightly in front of her.
There was a moment's silence and then
the first notes of the music began.
For as long as the girl could remember
music had seemed to tell her of
another world – a magical, exciting
world – that lay far, far away.
She always felt if she could just
close her eyes and lose herself,
then she would get there.
Maybe this time. As the music
swirled inside her, she swept
her arms above her head, rose on to
her toes and began to dance…*

At the Theatre

Rosa Maitland sat in the darkened theatre, her eyes fixed on the stage as Cinderella and Prince Charming danced together. Cinderella spun round, moving lightly across the stage. The Prince leaped into the air before sweeping her into an embrace.

Rosa glanced at her mother sitting beside

her in her wheelchair. There was a wistful
look on her mum's face and Rosa wondered
if she was remembering when she had once
been a ballerina and danced in theatres
around the world, before she'd had the
accident which had ended her dancing
career.

"Isn't this brilliant?" whispered Olivia,
Rosa's best friend, from the seat the other
side.

Rosa nodded. It was the best birthday treat ever! Her mum had got the three of them tickets to see the Petrovski Ballet Company. Rosa watched as the Prince spun Cinderella round for a final time and then Cinderella curtseyed and everyone in the audience broke into a storm of applause.

One day that will be me! Rosa thought, clapping as hard as she could. She loved dancing and went to classes three times a week at Madame Za-Za's ballet school. Her mum helped her practise between classes too.

And Rosa didn't just dance in class and at home. She had a secret. She had a pair of red ballet shoes that were magic and whisked her away to the land of Enchantia, a place where all the characters from the ballets lived. Rosa had had an amazing adventure there recently and she really hoped she would go back again soon.

As the curtain fell for the last time, lights came up in the auditorium and one of the theatre staff came to help Rosa's mum get her wheelchair out. All around them people started to stand up.

"That was amazing!" Olivia said as they all went out into the foyer. "Thank you so much for bringing me."

Rosa's mother smiled. "It's a pleasure, Olivia. They're a wonderful dance company. Their choreographer is Mikhail Gorbachevski. I danced with him many years ago."

"Really!" Olivia's eyes were wide. "Wow!"

"I'll show you both some pictures when we get home," said Mrs Maitland. "But first let's find a taxi."

Just as they reached the door of the theatre, Rosa heard someone call her mum's name in a Russian accent. "Eleanore! Eleanore Maitland!"

Her mum looked round.

A tall, slim man with dark hair and a grey jacket was coming towards them through the crowds.

Rosa's mother gasped. "Mikhail!"

The man took her hands and kissed her on both cheeks. "How wonderful to see you, Eleanore."

"And you." Rosa's mother smiled. "Girls, this is Mikhail who I was just telling you about." She turned back to the man. "Mikhail, this is my daughter, Rosa, and her friend, Olivia."

"Your daughter." Mikhail's eyes swept over Rosa. "She looks like you, Eleanore." He smiled at both the girls. "Did you enjoy the ballet?"

"Oh yes!" Rosa exclaimed. "It was brilliant!"

Olivia just nodded, seemingly lost for words at meeting such a famous ballet star.

"I want to be a ballerina one day," Rosa told him.

Mikhail smiled at her. "Then I hope you are as talented as your mother. Maybe you will dance for me one day." He looked at Mrs Maitland. "I would love to stay and catch up, Eleanore, but I have a meeting. Maybe you would like to bring the girls back to see *The Firebird* - the other ballet the company is performing? I can get you tickets." He pulled a wallet out of his jacket pocket and took out a card with his name and telephone number on it. "Let me know when you would like to come, and I will make sure I am free to meet up afterwards."

Rosa caught her breath. Now they would get to come to the ballet again! She turned to her mum in excitement. "Oh, wow! Wouldn't that be…"

"It's very kind of you, Mikhail," her

mum interrupted, "but I'm not sure we can manage it."

Mikhail looked surprised. "But you must."

Just then a taxi drew close. "Rosa could you get that taxi please?" Mrs Maitland said swiftly.

Wondering why her mum was being so strange, Rosa ran to ask the taxi driver to wait as her mum wheeled herself over.

"Here, let me help you," offered Mikhail as the taxi driver came round to let down a ramp to get the wheelchair into the back.

"I'll be fine, thank you," Rosa's mother said abruptly.

Mikhail's hands dropped from the chair.

The taxi driver shut the door and Mikhail came to the open window. "Goodbye, girls. Hopefully I will see you again at *The Firebird*." He looked at Rosa's mother. "Please come, Eleanore."

Mrs Maitland smiled stiffly and the taxi drove off.

"Oh, Mum! Can we go? Please!" Rosa said eagerly.

"We'll talk about it later. I'm tired." Mrs Maitland put a hand to her forehead.

Rosa sat back in her seat. *I'll talk to her tonight*, she decided. *She's got to say we can go… She's just got to!*

Enchantia Again!

"But why can't we?" Rosa demanded later that evening. Olivia had gone home and Rosa and her mum were talking about the ballet again. "Mikhail said we could have free tickets. You wouldn't have to pay."

"It's not about the money, Rosa," Mrs Maitland said briefly, busying herself in the kitchen with the washing up.

"So what is it about?" Rosa frowned, as her mum picked up a tea towel and started to dry the dishes.

She sighed. "It's complicated, sweetheart. I haven't kept in touch with any of my dancing friends because I don't want

them pitying me for not being able to dance when I don't pity myself. You see, I think of all the good things that have happened since the accident – like having you. But they wouldn't see it like that and I don't want free tickets

because they feel sorry for me."

Rosa thought about the man they had met at the theatre. "But Mikhail didn't seem to be offering you tickets because he felt sorry for you. He just said he wanted a chance to meet up."

"That may be what he said," Rosa's mother said, "but I think he felt differently." She sighed. "Look, it's late. Go and get ready for bed. I'm not going to talk about it any more."

Rosa couldn't believe her mum was going to turn the offer of tickets down because of this. "But Mum, what if Mikhail was just being nice and did just want to see you!" she said in frustration.

"Bed, Rosa!" her mum said.

Rosa knew that when her mum spoke that firmly there was no point arguing and so she turned and left the room. As she reached the door she glanced back. Her mum was staring at Mikhail's card, turning it over in her hand.

That night in bed, Rosa opened her *Stories from the Ballet* book and turned to the chapter on *The Firebird*. The ballet was about a princess who had been imprisoned by a magician. Whenever anyone tried to rescue her, the magician turned them to stone. But then one day a prince came along with a magical feather from a firebird which he used to rescue the princess and

turn the stone statues back into people.
Rosa shut her eyes, imagining what it
would be like to watch someone dance the
part of the Firebird…

She drifted off to sleep, dreaming of
fantastic birds and stone statues. When she
woke up a little while later, it was dark and
there was a faint tinkling sound as if

someone was playing a piano very softly.
Where was it coming from?

She sat up in bed and gasped. The red
ballet shoes at the bottom of
her bed were sparkling!
Rosa leaped up. This
must mean she was going
to Enchantia again! She pulled
on the shoes excitedly. Who would she
meet this time? What would she do?

As she tied the last ribbon, colours
started to whirl around her. She felt herself
spinning round and round, lifting into the
air.

After a few moments later she landed
back on the ground. The sparkles cleared
and the music stopped.

Rosa was standing in a wood. She could see the Royal Palace through the trees. There were butterflies flying around, rabbits hopping about and squirrels running up tree trunks. She spun round in excitement and then stopped. Something wasn't quite right. She looked around. What was it?

Suddenly she realised that there were no birds singing. The woods were silent. *That's weird*, she thought.

She looked at the palace in the distance. The last time she'd come to Enchantia she'd met Nutmeg, a helpful fairy. Maybe she should go to the palace and see if Nutmeg was there with the King and Queen.

Rosa set off. After she had been walking for about five minutes she heard the sound of voices carrying through the still air. They were raised and angry. Through the trees, she saw a small group of people. One of them was a slim fairy in a pale pink and brown tutu. *Nutmeg!*

Rosa's heart leaped at the sight of her

friend. She began to run but as she got closer, she saw that the group were arguing with a large fairy wearing a black dress and a long cloak. Her grey hair was in a bun and she had a hooked nose and warts. She looked very scary. Rosa stopped at the edge of the clearing.

"Please let the Firebird go," one of the men in the group was pleading with her.

"No!" snapped the fairy.

"But you can't just keep him in a cage. It's mean and the birds in the forest need to be able to sing again!" said Nutmeg. "You have to release him!"

The fairy glared at her. "*Have* to! No one tells me *I* have to do anything. I will do exactly as I please!"

"No you won't!" cried Nutmeg. She stepped forward towards the fairy. "We'll stop you!"

"Oh you will, will you? Well, we'll soon see about that!" The fairy laughed, a sound like breaking glass. "You impudent little fool! How dare you speak to me like that!"

She waved her long black wand. There was a flash of light and a loud crack.

Rosa's hands flew to her mouth. The people in front of the fairy were suddenly as still as statues. She had turned them all to stone!

The Fairy's Plan

The fairy threw her head back and laughed triumphantly. "I told you that you couldn't stop me!" And with that, she disappeared in a flash of green smoke.

Rosa ran into the clearing, her heart pounding.

"Nutmeg?" Rosa whispered, touching her friend's cold *grey* hand. "Nutmeg, are

you OK?" But Nutmeg's face was frozen in a shocked expression.

Tears welled up in Rosa's eyes. She couldn't believe what had just happened. Nutmeg had been turned to stone! Who was the horrid fairy? What had everyone been arguing with her about?

There's something going on in Enchantia and the shoes must have brought me here to help, thought Rosa.

"I'll go to the palace straight away," Rosa told Nutmeg, in case the fairy could still hear her. She squeezed

Nutmeg's stone fingers. "Don't worry. I'll try and sort this out. I promise!"

Running through the trees as fast as she could, she set off towards the Royal Palace. She headed down the main forest path until the trees came to an end. The palace was close by now. She raced towards the gates.

"Rosa!" the guard called. "The King and Queen were hoping you would come!"

He quickly let her in and showed her up to the royal parlour.

"Oh, Rosa! We're so glad to see you!" Queen Isabella exclaimed. She was sitting on the edge of the sofa, wringing her hands while King Tristan paced up and down.

"Enchantia is in desperate trouble," said the King.

"I saw a horrible fairy in the wood!" gasped Rosa. "She turned people to stone. Including Nutmeg!" She told the King and Queen what she had seen.

"That was the Wicked Fairy," said the King. "The same Wicked Fairy who once made our daughter, Princess Aurelia, prick her finger on a spinning wheel and fall asleep. Delphie helped to save her."

"The Wicked Fairy is horrible," said the Queen. "All the trouble at the moment is down to her."

"Why? What's going on?" burst out Rosa.

"The Wicked Fairy wants her palace to be the most talked about castle in the whole of Enchantia," King Tristan explained. "So she's been hanging cages filled with birds all around it. She sets traps and captures as many of them as she can – finches, robins, bluebirds, thrushes..."

"But the birds refused to sing in captivity," the Queen put in. "The Wicked Fairy got very angry and said that if they wouldn't sing for her then no one else

would hear any birds anywhere. So she captured the Firebird. He's part of the magic here. As long as he is free, the birds can sing and music can be played but when he is imprisoned, his magic fades so all the song and music in the land fades too."

"She's keeping him in a cage at the top of the tallest tree in Enchantia," said King Tristan. "Many brave people have tried to reach him or reason with her but she just turns them all to stone."

Just like the magician in the ballet of The Firebird, Rosa thought in alarm.

"We don't know what to do," the King went on worriedly. "There's a legend that says that if the Firebird is trapped but someone can get a feather from his tail and dance with it then he will be freed, but right now even if someone could get a feather it wouldn't be much use."

"Music and dance are linked in Enchantia," Queen Isabella explained. "Without music we simply can't dance. Look!" the Queen stood up and tried to pirouette forward, but she just stumbled and lost her balance. "Now the music has faded no one here is able to dance at all!"

Rosa frowned, remembering how she had twirled round in the woods when she had first got there. "That's strange. I think *I* can

still dance." She stood up and ran five tiny steps forward before pirouetting and then standing on one leg. She balanced perfectly.

The King and Queen gasped.

"Perhaps it's because I'm not actually from Enchantia," said Rosa. A thought suddenly struck her. "If I can get a feather from the Firebird and dance with it, then he will be free." She looked at them in excitement. "Where is he?"

"He's near the Wicked Fairy's palace which is a carriage ride away," said the King.

"It would be very dangerous to go there – the Wicked Fairy might turn you to stone!" said the Queen.

"I'll risk it!" Rosa said bravely.

"Oh, Rosa, I really don't know," said Queen Isabella worriedly.

"I must!" said Rosa. "The shoes have brought me here so I can help. I have to go. If you won't lend me a carriage, I'll just set off on my own!"

The King hesitated and then nodded. "Rosa has clearly made up her mind," he said, taking his wife's hand. "Let us at least give her what protection we can." He turned to Rosa. "If you are sure you want to go, I will call you a carriage and driver straight away."

Rosa lifted her chin. "I do. I want to go. I'm going to free the Firebird and save Enchantia. The Wicked Fairy isn't going to stop me!"

Traps in the Trees

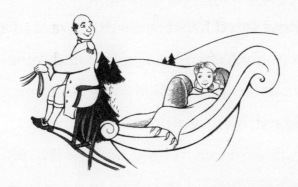

It was getting chilly as Rosa pulled the rugs in the carriage around her. Now the journey had started she began to wonder how it was going to end. How *was* she going to rescue the Firebird? What if she met the Wicked Fairy and was turned to stone like everyone else?

A picture of the Wicked Fairy's pale face

swam into Rosa's head and she shivered. She had felt so brave back at the palace, but now she could feel doubts filling her mind. *What if I can't help this time?* she thought anxiously. *What if I fail? How am I going to get a feather from the Firebird's tail?*

The driver – Griff – looked over his shoulder at her. "I used to know Delphie, the girl who had the ballet shoes before you," he said.

Rosa smiled. He was talking about Delphie Durand – the dark-haired girl at Madame Za-Za's ballet school who had given Rosa the red ballet shoes when she could no longer wear them.

"She's one of my friends," Rosa smiled. "She's really nice, isn't she?"

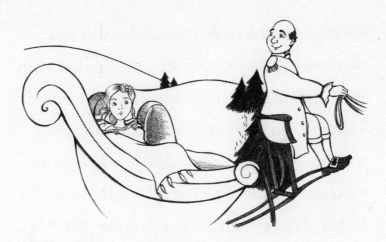

"Oh yes," Griff said. "Nice and brave. And such a lovely girl. It always seemed like she could solve every problem."

Rosa swallowed. *Delphie would have thought of a plan by now*, she thought.

"She always came up with some idea that could help," Griff went on. "So what's your plan for rescuing the Firebird then?"

"I'm... I'm not sure," Rosa admitted, feeling like a bit of a let down.

"Oh." Griff looked a bit surprised but then shrugged. "Well, I'm sure you'll think of something by the time we get there."

He turned back to look at the horses. *He's probably wishing Delphie was here instead of me*, thought Rosa. Pulling the rug around her, she stared at the countryside whizzing past. She hoped she'd think of something soon!

The horses cantered past fields and villages till at last they reached a wood of tall trees. There, Rosa could see strange wooden contraptions, like cages, made from branches. "What are they?" she asked.

"They're the bird traps set by the Wicked Fairy," Griff said grimly. "She's captured most of the birds in this wood already." The horses shook their heads nervously.

Rosa stared at the empty cages, thinking of all the birds the Wicked Fairy had captured and hoping no more would be caught. Suddenly her eyes were caught by a flash of blue in a cage halfway up a tree to her left. "Look!"

"It's a bird," Griff slowed the horses and peered through the trees. "A bluebird by the looks of it."

"We've got to let it out!" said Rosa. "What if the Wicked Fairy comes and takes it?"

"What if she comes and sees us here?" said Griff doubtfully. "If a bird is caught that probably means she'll be along soon to check the traps. We should get on our way."

But Rosa stood up. "No! I'm getting out! I'm going to rescue it!"

Almost before Griff had halted the horses, Rosa had scrambled down from the carriage. She hurried off the path, jumping over tree roots and ducking under branches until she reached the tree. A small bluebird with turquoise feathers and shining dark eyes was trapped inside the cage.

"Help!" he called, flapping his wings in alarm.

"Don't worry," called Rosa. "I'm coming!" She started to climb the tree, standing on tiptoe to grab the lowest branch with both hands and pulling herself up. Once on that branch she climbed up to another and another.

She looked at the door of the cage. It was fiddly to undo – a bird would never be able to manage it with its beak, but she could just about do it with her fingers – and pulled it open.

The bird opened its mouth, as if about to sing in delight, but no song came out. Instead, he swooped out and perched on her shoulder. "Oh, thank you! Thank you!" He butted his little head against her cheek. "I know I should never have flown into the woods but I was chasing a flying bug for my tea. I didn't see the cage until I flew inside. The door shut behind me and then I was trapped."

Rosa stroked his head. "You'd better get out of here. Just watch out for other traps on the way!"

She began to climb down the tree. The little bird flew after her. "My name's Skye."

"I'm Rosa."

"It's lovely to meet you, Rosa. I met Delphie once," said Skye. "She's lovely. So brave!"

There it was again – that same word. *Brave.* Rosa bit her lip. She wished people would stop telling her how amazing Delphie was. It wasn't making her feel very good by comparison.

"Are you going to rescue the Firebird?" Skye asked. "Can I come with you?"

"Thanks but I'd better go on my own. It'll be really dangerous," said Rosa.

51

"I don't mind," cheeped Skye. "I'd like to come and help."

"No," Rosa insisted. She would have loved the little bird's company, but what if they met the Wicked Fairy and he was caught? "You should get out of here. Go somewhere safe."

"But…"

"Rosa! We should go!" Griff called to her.

"Coming! Bye, Skye!" Rosa ran back to the carriage, waving back to the little bluebird. "Watch out for those cages!"

"But… but…" the little bird twittered.

Griff brought the reins down on the horses' backs and they leaped forward. "We'd best be off. It's too dangerous to stay here and the Firebird needs to be freed," he said.

Rosa felt as if Griff was telling her off for stopping to rescue Skye. *He probably thinks Delphie wouldn't have stopped,* she thought. Sighing, she pulled the rugs up around her and set her mind to thinking what she would do to free the Firebird. She had to think of something – and fast!

In the Clearing

The rest of the journey passed in silence. A few times Rosa saw Griff start to turn towards her but she hastily shut her eyes as if she was dozing. She didn't want him starting to tell her how amazing he thought Delphie was again, particularly seeing as she was aware that she still hadn't thought of a plan!

She kept wracking her brains. How was she going to get up to its cage? What was she going to do if the Wicked Fairy was there?

She caught sight of a palace through the trees. It was made of grey stone and had black flags flying from its pointed turrets. All around it were cages full of birds.

Griff slowed the horses to a walk. "The tallest tree is close to the edge of the woods," he said. "It might be safer to walk the last bit in case the Wicked Fairy hears the horses coming."

Rosa swallowed nervously. This was it. They were here. Griff halted and she got down. There was a clearing a little way ahead of them, and in it were six stone statues, two princes on horses, a fairy, a girl dressed as a soldier and two princes on foot.

They must all be people who had tried to rescue the Firebird! She started to hurry towards the clearing.

"Be careful, Rosa!" Griff called in a low voice.

But Rosa ignored him. She wanted to get to the Firebird as quickly as possible. But, just as she reached the edge of the clearing, the Wicked Fairy appeared ahead of her!

Just in time, Rosa threw herself down behind a leafy bush. The Wicked Fairy swung around and looked suspiciously in her direction, as if she had heard a noise.

With her heart beating fast, Rosa realised that the bush was hollow in the middle. She quickly crawled inside, hoping Griff was hiding too. Branches caught in her hair and her fingernails dug into the soil but she took no notice. Her eyes were fixed on the Wicked Fairy who was stalking straight towards her!

As the Wicked Fairy reached the bush where she was hiding, Rosa hardly dared to breathe. *Please don't see me*, she thought. *Please!*

"Must just have been a bird," the Wicked Fairy muttered, cackling. "If it is, I'll catch it for my collection!" She marched back into the clearing and looked up towards something in the branches of one of the trees. "How are you enjoying your cage, Firebird?" she called out. "Get used to it because you'll be staying there for a long time!" And with that, she waved her wand and vanished in a flash.

Phew! thought Rosa as she crawled out from under the bush.

"Rosa, are you OK?"

She looked round and saw Griff coming out from behind a tree trunk. "You shouldn't have run ahead like that! You could have been caught!"

"I know, it was stupid!" The scare she had just had made Rosa speak more crossly than she would usually. "I bet Delphie would never have done anything like that, would she?"

Griff stared at her. "What do you mean?"

All the worry about not having thought of a plan yet and the fear that she wasn't as good as Delphie, spilled out of Rosa. "Well, it's clear you think Delphie would have

been more careful and that Delphie would have had a plan. You think she was *wonderful!*"

Griff looked astonished. "Yes, she was. But so are you. I've heard about your last adventure here and how you got into King

Rat's castle. That was incredible. And the way you insisted on rescuing Skye the bluebird. That was really brave too." He frowned. "I've only been talking about Delphie because I really liked her and you said you were friends. I didn't mean to

make it sound like Delphie was braver or better than you."

"Oh." Rosa went red as she realised that she had jumped to conclusions.

Griff looked upset.

Rosa swallowed, feeling bad for upsetting him. "I'm… I'm sorry," she said. "I got it wrong. I should have asked you what you meant."

Griff gave her a kindly smile. "That's all right. We both just got our wires crossed. Let's forget it now. There are far more important things to think about – like how to rescue the Firebird before the Wicked Fairy comes back. Look, there he is!"

Griff pointed up the tallest tree. A handsome prince had been turned to stone

right beside it, looking up into the branches.
Rosa saw a narrow cage hanging near the
very top. A bird about the size of an eagle
was shut inside.

It had beautiful
red and gold
feathers and a
proud face.

"The Firebird!"
Rosa breathed.

"He shouldn't
be trapped like
that. He should be
free," said Griff, stepping over a pile of
cloaks that had been discarded by people
as they had got ready to rescue the
Firebird.

"How are you going to get up there?" he said, walking up to the tree. "It looks impossible!"

Rosa remembered how she had just saved Skye. "I'll climb up."

"But there aren't any branches you can reach from here," Griff pointed out.

Rosa realised he was right. The lower part of the trunk was very smooth. The first branches were far out of reach, about five metres up the tree. It would be impossible to climb from the ground.

"If only we had a ladder," she said, looking around the clearing.

But there was nothing around that could help. Unless…

Her eyes fell on the statue of the prince near the trunk and widened as she thought of an idea. "Griff, could you climb on that statue? Then, if I climb up on your shoulders, I should be able to reach the first branch!"

Griff looked at the stone statue and then looked at the branches. "Yes, I could do that. I'm sure Prince Hugo wouldn't mind."

"I'm sorry, Prince Hugo," Rosa said quickly to the prince in case he could hear. It wasn't very dignified for a prince to be climbed on, but they had to rescue the Firebird and this was the only way she could think of.

Griff began to climb on to the prince's shoulders.

Once he was balanced, Rosa followed him up. It was a bit like being an acrobat in the circus! Griff bent down and she climbed on to his shoulders and then he straightened slowly up. She could almost reach the lowest branch, almost…

Griff wobbled. Rosa made a desperate grab and her fingers found a branch. Using all of her strength, she hauled herself up so her tummy was on the branch, and then pulled her legs up. Taking a deep breath, she began to climb.

It was very difficult. The branches were spaced out and thoughts of the Wicked Fairy kept filling Rosa's mind. What if she

came back and saw Rosa halfway up the
tree? There would be no way to hide from
her there.

Rosa glanced
down. The ground
was a long way off
now. A wave of
dizziness swept
over her. She
clutched the
trunk, feeling
like she was

going to fall. *Don't stop, don't stop*, she told
herself. But suddenly her arms and legs felt
as if they wouldn't work.

I can't do it, she thought in panic. *I can't!*

"Go on, Rosa!" urged Griff from below.

Rosa took courage from his voice. Everyone in Enchantia needed her to do this. She wasn't going to give up!

Gritting her teeth, she edged further up the tree. She'd gone a few more metres when suddenly her feet slipped. For a moment she swung in mid-air, her hands locked round a branch before she regained her footing and edged back towards the trunk to pause, trembling and clinging on.

She shut her eyes, blinking back the tears. *You have to keep going*, she told herself and taking a deep breath, she began to climb again...

Rescued!

"Rosa!"

Rosa looked round and gasped. Skye, the little bluebird, was swooping towards her.

"Skye!" she gasped. "What are you doing here? I told you not to come."

"But I thought you might need help. I tried to keep up with the carriage, but I couldn't – I needed to fly carefully because of the traps. Anyway, I'm here now!" Skye flew closer, his dark eyes concerned. "Are you all right?"

"Not really," Rosa said, hanging on to the tree trunk. "I've got to get up to the Firebird."

The bluebird looked worried. "I could fly up there but I won't be able to undo his cage with my beak."

"I don't need to do undo the cage," Rosa said quickly. "I just need one of his tail feathers."

"I can easily get one of those for you!" said Skye.

"Really?" said Rosa, her heart jumping.

"Of course! Watch me!" Skye flew upwards.

Rosa watched the little bird fly all the
way to the cage. He chirruped something to
the Firebird who nodded his elegant head.
The bluebird gently
plucked one of the
red-gold feathers out of
his long tail, then
whizzed back
down to Rosa
with it.

"You've got
it!" she gasped.
She longed to take the shining feather, but
first she had to get back down the tree. She
began the long, slow climb down, her feet
slowly finding footholds, her arms trembling
with the strain.

"Rosa!" she heard Griff shout from below. "Jump!"

Rosa glanced down. Griff had made a hammock with the discarded cloaks! He had strung it between the statue of Prince Hugo and a nearby statue of a man on a horse. If she jumped, she would land in it and then she would be on the ground and could do the dance!

"Come on," urged Griff again.

"Go on, Rosa!" said Skye.

Taking a deep breath, Rosa jumped. For a few brief seconds she felt the air whizzing past, saw the blue sky overhead, and thought she was going to crash into the ground. But then she landed in the hammock. She bounced upwards and down

again, as if she was on a trampoline!

She blinked as her bouncing slowed down. Griff was grinning at her.

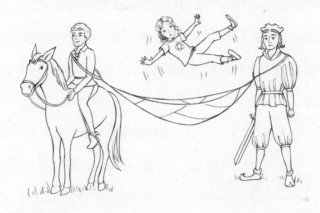

"Thanks!" she gasped, swinging her legs over the side and tumbling out.

Skye swooped down. "Here's the feather, Rosa!"

Rosa took it gratefully and ran to the centre of the clearing. Now all she had to do was dance. But which should she perform?

Then she remembered what she had watched the dancers doing the night before at the theatre.

She raised her arms above her head, crossed her left leg behind her right and then ran forward, bringing her arms down so they were just slightly behind her. She pirouetted and danced forward another step before balancing on her toes. Then she circled round the statues, turning with every step, arms out to the sides, the feather

whisking through the air. As she turned
and spun, she heard the faint sound of
birdsong! She stopped in an arabesque, one
leg out behind her and looked at Skye. The
little bird had his mouth open and notes
were starting to pour out.
He flapped his wings in
delight. "I'm singing
again!"

Rosa spun on again and suddenly music
started to fill the clearing. She got faster
and faster as the music grew louder and
stronger. Acting instinctively, she brushed
the feather against the statues. As soon as
the feather touched the first one, the stone
on all of them started to crack and they
began to turn back into real people. The

music reached a peak and there was a loud
BANG!

Rosa stopped, her gaze flying upwards.
The bottom of the cage had burst open
and the Firebird was
swooping out and
into the air, free at
last! The cage
came away from
the branch and
started to fall
when suddenly
there was a piercing,
furious shriek…

Rosa turned to see the Wicked Fairy
rushing into the clearing!

The Firebird's Feather

"What's happening?" the Wicked Fairy screamed. She looked up and saw the Firebird in the sky. "NO!" Her eyes fell on Rosa and took in the red shoes and the feather in her hand. "You! This is *your* fault!"

Rosa shrank back, her blood running icy with fear.

The Wicked Fairy lifted her wand. "Just you wait…"

She broke off with a shriek as the narrow cage above her plummeted down from the sky, falling straight over her head and snapping her wand.

"What the… what the…" The Wicked Fairy stared out from behind the bars. She began to waddle around, the cage reaching all the way down to her ankles. "I'm trapped! Get me out of here!" she yelled furiously. "GET ME OUT!"

"No way," cried Rosa.

"You trapped the Firebird in there! Now see how you like it!"

The Wicked Fairy jumped up and down with rage. But no one was about to help her.

"I'll get you all for this!" she cursed, stamping away through the trees.

"I hope no one lets her out for a while!" Prince Hugo said.

Rosa grinned. She was sure the Wicked Fairy would find someone to take the cage off her at some point but right now it was good that she had a taste of her own medicine!

The fairy who had been a statue pirouetted over to Rosa. "I'm Sugar the Sugar Plum Fairy, Nutmeg's older sister. You set the Firebird free and saved the day!" She took Rosa's hands. "Now I will use my magic to take us back to the Royal Palace. They will all be celebrating there and the King and Queen will want to know what happened!"

Rosa's eyes flew to Griff.

"Don't worry about me," he said. "I'll head back with the carriage."

"And I'm going to see if I can find my family," said Skye flying down from up on high. "I've just been above the treetops and the cages at the Wicked Fairy's palace have burst open too. All the birds are free!"

"Brilliant!" Rosa gasped. She turned to Sugar. "Yes, please take me back."

But just as Sugar raised her wand, the Firebird swooped down into the clearing in a blaze of red and gold. Every feather on his body glittered and shone with magic and his dark eyes looked brightly at Rosa. "Thank you!" he called to Rosa. "You have brought music and song back to Enchantia."

Rosa smiled in delight, watching as he flew up into the sky, soaring above the trees, free once again.

Looking happily at the feather in her hand, she slipped it into her pyjama pocket.

Sugar grinned. "Come on. Your job here is done. Let's go back to the palace!"

Sugar waved her wand. Pink sparkles swirled around Rosa and the next second she felt herself being whisked away.

Back in the palace, everyone was celebrating, just as Sugar had said. Birds were perched on every part of the palace walls, singing sweetly as if to make up for the time they had been silent. A band was playing and people were dancing in the courtyard.

"Rosa! Sugar!"

Rosa swung round and saw Nutmeg pushing her way through the crowd. "What happened? All we know is that suddenly the spell broke and everyone was free."

"Let's go inside and Rosa can tell the King and Queen too," said Sugar and they hurried into the palace.

"I'm so glad you're all right," said Rosa to Nutmeg. "I saw you being turned into stone. It was awful."

"I'm OK. It didn't hurt," said Nutmeg. "And now everyone is fine, thanks to you!"

They got inside and Rosa told the King and Queen and Nutmeg what had happened.

"I couldn't have done it without Griff and Skye," she finished.

"They will be well rewarded," the King promised. "Now, come and join the dancing outside!"

But as he spoke, Rosa's shoes started to glow. "I've got to go!" she gasped.

"See you soon, Rosa!" called Nutmeg.

"Bye!" cried Rosa as she was whisked away.

She landed back in her bedroom in the dark. What an adventure! She could hardly believe everything that had just happened.

She untied her ballet shoes and then climbed into her bed, a minute later she was fast asleep.

Second Chances

The next morning she went downstairs, her fingers playing with the Firebird feather in her pocket. Her mum was in the kitchen getting out the breakfast things. Rosa took a deep breath. "Mum, I've been thinking about the tickets and I think you should ring Mikhail."

Her mum sighed. "We went through this

last night. I'm sorry if you're disappointed, love but…"

Rosa didn't let her finish. "Mum, it's not just because I want to go and see the ballet, although of course I do. I just think you really should ring Mikhail. I know you think that he's feeling sorry for you, but sometimes," and she thought about Griff, "well, we don't always get it right when we guess what other people are thinking, and you said you and he were friends."

Rosa held her breath, wondering what her mum would say.

Her mum stared. "Where did all that come from?"

Rosa shrugged. "I don't know. I was just thinking about it. You should find out what

Mikhail's really thinking and not just guess. You're always telling me not to judge people." She looked hopefully at her mum. "Please will you ring him?"

A smile caught at her mum's mouth. "I can't argue with that. You're right. Maybe I shouldn't jump to conclusions. Perhaps I have got it wrong."

Rosa's eyes widened. "So you'll ring?"

Her mum hesitated and then nodded.

"I will. And if he offers me tickets again, I'll say yes."

Rosa spun round joyfully. She was sure her mum was just as mistaken about Mikhail as she had been about Griff. "Oh wow!" she gasped. "Just wait until I tell Olivia!"

Two weeks later, Rosa sat in the auditorium of the theatre with her mum, Mikhail and Olivia. From the moment they had met up with him before the show, he and Rosa's mother had been laughing and talking, catching up on lost time. Every seat was filled. The stage was blazing with light as a dancer dressed in a red and gold costume leaped across the stage, arms thrown back like a bird in flight.

Rosa pictured the real Firebird soaring through the sky in Enchantia. When would she go back there again? She put her hand in the pocket of her skirt and her fingers closed around the feather. *Soon,* she thought. And she smiled.

Darcey's Magical Masterclass

The Firebird's Flight

The Firebird is an amazing creature that flies all over Enchantia!
Try this springing step and imagine that you are the Firebird starting
to take flight, remember to flap those arms like wings!

1.
Start in the 3rd position, with your left foot behind your right foot and your arms in the prepare position.

2.
Bend your knees.

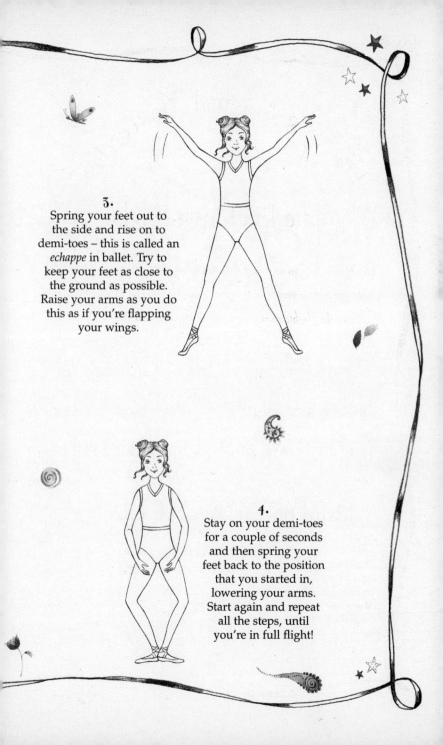

3.
Spring your feet out to the side and rise on to demi-toes – this is called an *echappe* in ballet. Try to keep your feet as close to the ground as possible. Raise your arms as you do this as if you're flapping your wings.

4.
Stay on your demi-toes for a couple of seconds and then spring your feet back to the position that you started in, lowering your arms. Start again and repeat all the steps, until you're in full flight!

Magic Ballerina™

Rosa and the Magic Moonstone

The magical moonstone of Enchantia has broken and all of the ballets have become muddled up! Can Rosa put things right?

Read on for a sneak preview of book nine...

The air filled with music and the curtains started to open, revealing a brightly lit stage. A girl in a nightdress danced on. Maybe it's Clara from *The Nutcracker*, thought Rosa, wondering what was happening. But then she saw that the girl wasn't holding a nutcracker doll, she was holding a pumpkin! She was followed by a group of soldiers who looked like they were also from *The Nutcracker*. They were fighting a group of dancing giant sweets. *But in the ballet they fight an army of mice*, thought Rosa.

Before she had time to say anything, the soldiers had danced off the stage and a girl in rags had come on. *Cinderella!* thought Rosa. A beautiful fairy spun on after her. But it wasn't Cinderella's Fairy Godmother, it was Sugar, the Sugar Plum Fairy! Two more people followed them. They were dancing a *pas de deux*. One of them was a beautiful girl with long dark hair who looked like Sleeping Beauty. Rosa stared.

Sleeping Beauty wasn't dancing with her handsome prince though; instead she was dancing with a surprised-looking Puss In Boots!

What's going on? Rosa wondered. All the ballets seem to be completely mixed up!

The curtain started to close. Rosa jumped to her feet. "Wait!" she called. She hurried out of her row of seats. But the curtains had shut.

°ⓞ·*·☆·ⓞ·*·☆·ⓞ·*·☆·ⓞ·*·°

Darcey Bussell

MBuy more great Magic Ballerina books direct from HarperCollins at 10% off recommended retail price.
FREE postage and packing in the UK.

Delphie and the Magic Ballet Shoes	ISBN 978 0 00 728607 2
Delphie and the Magic Spell	ISBN 978 0 00 728608 9
Delphie and the Masked Ball	ISBN 978 0 00 728610 2
Delphie and the Glass Slippers	ISBN 978 0 00 728617 1
Delphie and the Fairy Godmother	ISBN 978 0 00 728611 9
Delphie and the Birthday Show	ISBN 978 0 00 728612 6
Rosa and the Secret Princess	ISBN 978 0 00 730029 7
Rosa and the Golden Bird	ISBN 978 0 00 730030 3
Rosa and the Magic Moonstone	ISBN 978 0 00 730031 0
Rosa and the Special Prize	ISBN 978 0 00 730032 7
Rosa and the Magic Dream	ISBN 978 0 00 730033 4
Rosa and the Three Wishes	ISBN 978 0 00 730034 1

All priced at £3.99

To purchase by Visa/Mastercard/Switch simply call
08707871724 or fax on **08707871725**

To pay by cheque, send a copy of this form with a cheque made payable to
'HarperCollins Publishers' to: Mail Order Dept. (Ref: BOB4),
HarperCollins Publishers, Westerhill Road, Bishopbriggs, G64 2QT,
making sure to include your full name, postal address and phone number.

From time to time HarperCollins may wish to use your personal data
to send you details of other HarperCollins publications and offers.
If you wish to receive information on other HarperCollins publications
and offers please tick this box ☐

Do not send cash or currency. Prices correct at time of press.
Prices and availability are subject to change without notice.
Delivery overseas and to Ireland incurs a £2 per book postage and packing charge.